Milkman Mike

AND THE SPACESHIP

GREAT N ORTHERN

Great Northern Books
PO Box 1380, Bradford, West Yorkshire, BD5 5FB

www.greatnorthernbooks.co.uk

ISBN: 978-1-914227-41-7

Illustrated by Nicky Mills

CIP Data
A catalogue for this book is available from the British Library.

One day Milkman Mike was delivering his milk when suddenly he heard a buzz-buzz-buzz noise up in the sky.

BUZZ BUZZ BUZZ

Milkman Mike looked up and saw something big and yellow over Farmer Cream's field.

It looked like a big triangle of cheese with green spots. "What is that?" said Milkman Mike to Spike the big daft dog. Spike was in Milkman Mike's pickup called Gold Top 2.

What was it?
It was a spaceship!

Milkman Mike nearly dropped the milk bottles he was carrying.
"Hey, Spike!" said Milkman Mike.

But Spike didn't hear Milkman Mike because he was asleep. He was dreaming of
Milkman Mike's naughty runaway bottles and running after them.

Milkman Mike carried on delivering his milk.

The spaceship followed him.

The spaceship followed him to Miss Goodness's bakery where she was making her lovely lemon curds.

The spaceship followed him to the school where Milkman Mike delivered his milk for the schoolchildren.

GOODNESS BAKERY

SCHOOL

"Spike! Wake up!" said Milkman Mike.

But Spike had a smile on his face and stayed asleep.

"You big daft dog!" said Milkman Mike. "You are missing a spaceship!"

The spaceship came lower and slower until it was just above Farmer Cream's cows.

Farmer Cream had come out to see the spaceship.

Was Milkman Mike a little bit scared?

Yes, he was.

Was Farmer Cream a little bit scared?

Yes, he was, for his cows.

Was Spike a little bit scared?

No, because he was asleep, dreaming of naughty runaway bottles.

Suddenly the spaceship moved up and away from Farmer Cream's cows and went VROOOOM!

The spaceship had gone.

"Arr, arr, arr," said Spike, as he woke up, yawning and stretching. "Have you seen a spaceship?"

"How do you know I've seen a spaceship?" said Mike.

"Arr, arr, arr," said Spike.

"Dogs know everything."

"Arr, arr, arr ... maybe,"
said Spike, shaking his head.
"I don't like spaceships."

Also available in the Milkman Mike series

Milkman Mike and the Runaway Bottles

Milkman Mike and the Fire Engine

Milkman Mike and the Football Match

www.greatnorthernbooks.co.uk